Canoe Days

Gary Paulsen

Illustrated by
Ruth Wright Paulsen

Dragonfly Books ———— New York

Visit us on the Web! www.randomhouse.com/kids

Educators and librarians, for a variety of teaching tools, visit us at www.randomhouse.com/teachers

The Library of Congress has cataloged the hardcover edition of this work as follows:

Paulsen, Gary.
Canoe days / Gary Paulsen ; illustrated by Ruth Wright Paulsen.
p. cm.
Summary: A canoe ride on a northern lake during a summer day reveals the quiet beauty and wonder of nature in and around the peaceful water.
ISBN 978-0-585-32524-0 (trade)
[1. Nature—Fiction. 2. Summer—Fiction.] I. Paulsen, Ruth Wright, ill. II. Title.
PZ7.P2843Ca   In 1998
[E]—dc21
97021542

ISBN 978-0-440-41441-4 (pbk.)

MANUFACTURED IN CHINA

16 15 14 13 12 11 10 9 8 7

First Dragonfly Books Edition

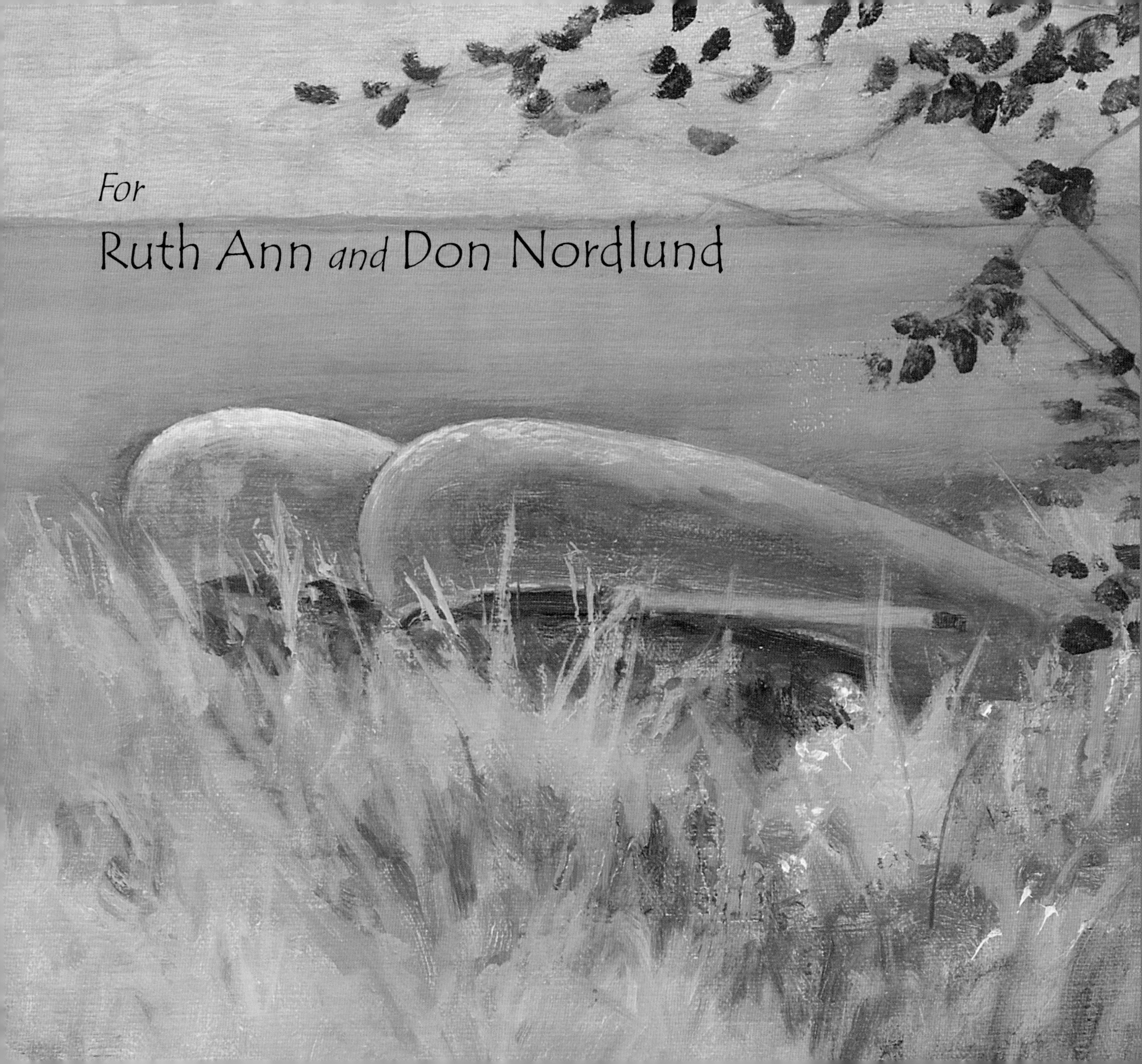

For

Ruth Ann *and* Don Nordlund

Sometimes when it is still,
so still you can hear the swish
of a butterfly's wing—

sometimes when it is that still I take the canoe out on the edge of the lake.

One stroke of the paddle and we are gone, the canoe and me, moving silently.

Across water so quiet it becomes part of the sky, the canoe slides in green magic without a ripple, disappears like a ghost floating in the airwater over the playground where fish play.

The water is a window into the skylake.

Sunfish under lily pads living in cool green rooms, watching for water bugs to make a lunch. Watching for frogs to make a dinner.

But still now, everything frozen while the cold slash of a hunting northern pike moves like an arrow through the pads, looking, fiercely searching always for something to eat; and then he's gone into the green depths.

Ahead is a mallard hen, her ducklings spread out like a spotted fan around her looking for skittering oar bugs to eat. The canoe does not frighten her—she does not see the man, only the canoe, as a shiny log floating in the sun.

And there a fawn, on the edge, his feet in the water, ears flopping the flies away while he watches the canoe glide past, as unafraid as the mallard.

But his mother is near, in the bush, knowing better and trying to get him away with short stamps of her feet.

Come away now. Come away *now*.

A fox drinks, soft laps with a pink tongue while
the paddle waits, all still. Then the fox slips away.

A raccoon turns a log looking for worms to eat.

A snake moves from
shore to pad, a wavy ripple, green back and
light belly making it invisible when it stops.

And then, perfect on the brim of my cap, a dragonfly catches a deerfly that would have bitten me and eats there without leaving;

while I hold my breath and see the fawn and the ducks and the doe and the snake and the frogs and the fish and the fox and the badger all around me while the sun is on my back like a golden friend on this perfect day.

A canoe day.